DiNKiN DiNGS

AND THE
FRIGHTENING THINGS

To Ruth and Ian, and to things that go bump in the night ~ GB

To my parents ~ PW

Check out Dinkin's Bebo page at:
www.bebo.com/dinkindings

GROSSET & DUNLAP
Published by the Penguin Group
Penguin Group (USA) Inc., 375 Hudson Street, New York, New York 10014, USA
Penguin Group (Canada), 90 Eglinton Avenue East, Suite 700, Toronto, Ontario M4P
2Y3, Canada (a division of Pearson Penguin Canada Inc.)
Penguin Books Ltd., 80 Strand, London WC2R 0RL, England
Penguin Group Ireland, 25 St. Stephen's Green, Dublin 2, Ireland
(a division of Penguin Books Ltd.)
Penguin Group (Australia), 250 Camberwell Road, Camberwell, Victoria 3124, Australia
(a division of Pearson Australia Group Pty. Ltd.)
Penguin Books India Pvt. Ltd., 11 Community Centre, Panchsheel Park,
New Delhi – 110 017, India
Penguin Group (NZ), 67 Apollo Drive, Rosedale, North Shore 0632, New Zealand
(a division of Pearson New Zealand Ltd.)
Penguin Books (South Africa) (Pty.) Ltd., 24 Sturdee Avenue,
Rosebank, Johannesburg 2196, South Africa

Penguin Books Ltd., Registered Offices: 80 Strand, London WC2R 0RL, England

Text copyright © 2009 Guy Bass. Illustrations copyright © 2009 Pete Williamson. First published in Great Britain in 2009 by Stripes Publishing. First published in the United States in 2011 by Grosset & Dunlap, a division of Penguin Young Readers Group, 345 Hudson Street, New York, New York 10014. GROSSET & DUNLAP is a trademark of Penguin Group (USA) Inc. Printed in the U.S.A.

Library of Congress Cataloging-in-Publication Data is available.

ISBN 978-0-448-45431-3 (pbk)   10 9 8 7 6 5 4 3 2 1
ISBN 978-0-448-45432-0 (HC)   10 9 8 7 6 5 4 3 2

DiNKiN DiNGS

AND THE

FRIGHTENING THINGS

GUY BASS

ILLUSTRATED BY
PETE WiLLiaMSON

Grosset & Dunlap
An Imprint of Penguin Group (USA) Inc.

THE THING ABOUT DINKIN DINGS

Dinkin Dings was afraid of everything. And not just actual scary things, like getting stuck in an elevator with a hungry tiger or pushed out of an airplane with only a tissue for a parachute. No, he was afraid of pretty much, absolutely, and totally everything. Dinkin could find reasons to be scared of things that weren't scary at all.

Here are his forty-seven most terrifying things as of 9:19 on May 19:

Fairgrounds,
loud sounds,
busy neighborhoods and towns,
computer games,
goofy names,
polished, wooden picture frames,
road signs,
straight lines,
breakfast, lunch, and dinnertimes,
lamp posts,
cold toast,
sweaters worn by game-show hosts,
garbage cans and their garbage can lids,
sheep and goats (and lambs and kids),
telephones,
microphones,
whispers,
sisters,
moans and groans,
smelly feet,
rotten meat,

crosswords that are incomplete,

trees,

peas,

knees,

fleas,

laser-guided killer bees,

carpet stains,

busy trains,

elephants with robot brains,

prison bars,

haunted cars,

7

every sort of thing from Mars,

doors,

chores,

dinosaurs (especially

ones that live indoors),

the art of mime,

mutant slime,

and lists of things

that seem to rhyme.

In fact, there were only three things that Dinkin wasn't afraid of.

He wasn't afraid of The Frightening Things.

SECRET, INVISIBLE KILLER SHARKS AND OTHER BATH TIME PERILS

Risk of drowning: 18%
Risk of shampoo-in-the-eye: 65%
Risk of secret, invisible killer sharks: 91.7%

"Dinkin! Time for your bath!" called Dinkin's mother, knocking on his bedroom door. It was four minutes after eight in the evening on the eleventh hottest day of the year.

"I'm not ready yet!" said Dinkin as Mrs. Dings opened the door. There was Dinkin in a pair of red swimming trunks, with water wings on each arm and leg. He was wearing a homemade breathing apparatus made from a plastic bottle, part of an old hose, and an entire roll of packing tape.

"The Bath-Buster 2.0 hasn't even been

tested—what if it malfunctions? I could drown!" he said through his breathing mask.

"I'm sure it'll be fine," said Mrs. Dings, hurrying Dinkin into the bathroom.

"Did you check for poisonous jellyfish?" mumbled Dinkin.

"Yes," said his mom.

"And sharks? Did you check for sharks?"

"Dinkin, dear, I think you'd know if there was a shark in your bath."

"What if it were an invisible shark? An invisible killer shark that escaped from a secret, invisible laboratory that makes secret, invisible killer sharks," said Dinkin.

"Oh, I think your father checked for invisible sharks," said his mom.

"Did he use the De-Invisibilizer?" said Dinkin suspiciously.

"Of course I did," said Dinkin's dad cheerfully, appearing at the bathroom door. "I de-invisibilized the whole house this morning. Didn't I, Mrs. Dings?"

11

"You did, Mr. Dings," replied Mrs. Dings, crossing her fingers behind her back. She had no idea what a De-Invisibilizer was —she could never keep up with Dinkin's inventions. In the last week alone, he had created:

-the Anti-Sub-Atomizer Belt (to protect against spontaneous shrinkage)

-the Void-Avoider (for the prevention of sudden other-dimensional entrapment)

-the Insect Detector-Inspector-Deflector (for the detection, inspection, and deflection of all insects— except weevils, which naturally required the Weevils-Upheaval attachment)

-the Anti-Everything Machine (which, due to various explosions, was still in the development stage)

All of Dinkin's inventions seemed to be held together with sticky tape and string, and made from anything he could get his hands on, from liquid soap bottles to hair dryers to bicycle pumps.

"Well, as long as you de-invisibilized

everywhere," said Dinkin, climbing carefully into the bath while using his not-quite-waterproof Aquat-O-Meter to scan for possible bath-related threats.

"Don't be too long," said Mr. Dings. "We don't want you turning into a prune."

"*Turning into a prune*?!" squealed Dinkin. There were several things that Dinkin was terrified of turning into, including a fork, a snail, and a cloud. But a prune sounded like the worst thing of all! Dinkin washed himself in exactly twenty-two-and-a-half seconds, then leaped from the bath and dried off.

"A prune!" he said. "Why does no one warn you about these things? Danger is everywhere!"

And it was six seconds later that Dinkin heard The Sound of the End of the World.

NEW NEIGHBORS

Chance of rain: 27%
Chance of world ending: 65%

GRRRRAAUUUUuu
¹⁴MMBFSSCHCHHHHh!

After hearing The Sound of the End of the World, Dinkin fled to his room and locked himself in his Fortress of Ultimate Protection. The fortress may have looked like four cardboard boxes tied together with string, but it was the only place in the world that Dinkin ever got close to feeling safe.

"IT'S THE END OF THE WORLD!"

15

Dinkin had read all about the end of the world at the library. In a dusty copy of the 1969 *Encyclopedia Scaremonger*, he had discovered that:

1) The Sound of the End of the World will sound (or at least be spelled) like this:

GrRRrAAUUUUUU-MMBFSSCHCH!

2) The Sound of the End of the World will warn of The End of the World, but will come without warning.

3) The Sound of the End of the World will finally be followed by The Actual, Real-Life End of the World.*

* Subject to change without notice. The Sound of the End of the World does not guarantee delivery of the End of the World. The World accepts no responsibility for loss or damages to your stuff as a result of the End of the World.

"It's all right, Dinkin," said Mr. Dings, coming into Dinkin's room. He peered out the window to the street below. "It's just a moving van pulling in next door."

"Moving van?" whispered Dinkin. He peered out from inside the fortress.

"Yes, it's our new neighbors," said Mr. Dings. "You remember . . . our last neighbors decided to move after you kept laying traps in their garden."

"They were bears!" cried Dinkin. "Bears disguised as people! It was *so* obvious! What was I supposed to do? Let them eat us?"

"Well, I hope you're not thinking of accusing anyone else of being a bear. You got us into an awful lot of trouble last time," said Mr. Dings with a long sigh. Then something caught his eye. "Hey, Dinkin, look!"

"What? What?!" said Dinkin. He crept over to the window on his hands and knees, then popped his nose onto the windowsill and peered out.

17

All he could see was the moving van in the driveway, looking very much like an enormous, sleeping monster.

"It looks like our new neighbors have a daughter!" said Mr. Dings. Dinkin squinted. There, in the front garden, was a *girl*. She looked younger than Dinkin. She had blond pigtails and a missing front tooth, and was wearing a T-shirt which said 100% PONY CRAZY on the front in fat, pink letters. She was playing with a small, brown dog.

"Isn't that wonderful?" said Mr. Dings.

"You can make a new friend!"

But Dinkin was already fearing the worst. Girls were scary enough as it was. Dinkin took one look at that girl and realized it was much worse than he could ever have imagined. That girl wasn't a girl at all. She was something much, much more terrifying.

THiS WAS A JOB FOR THE FRiGHTENiNG THiNGS!

19

ENTER THE FRIGHTENING THINGS

Actual time: 12:01 AM
Dinkin time: horror o'clock

20 Dinkin sat awake in his bed. It was one minute since he had recited the Ancient Summoning Chant. Would his friends get here in time to save him?

"Where are they?" he whispered, fear gripping him like a hand around his throat. Suddenly, his bedroom window began to rattle like a snake's tail. His closet door creaked slowly, as if something was trying to escape from inside. From under his bed came a low growl, like the sound of rolling thunder.

Dinkin stared as something crawled out from under the bed. The latch on his window popped open, and a freezing, moaning wind swept into the room. The closet door swung on its hinges with a creak, and he heard the rattle of dry bones. As Dinkin felt the shapes loom over him, he reached out a trembling hand for the bedside lamp and turned it on.

It was the stuff of nightmares! To his left was a ghostly apparition, floating in the air and wailing a bloodcurdling wail. To his right was a hideous, fat monster, with skin as green and scaly as a crocodile's neck, and sharp, yellowing tusks.

And a living skeleton, with eyes like two bottomless pits and long, bony fingers. Dinkin stared at the creatures before him, his eyes wide.

"What took you so long?" he said. "I summoned you *ages* ago."

"Sorry, Dinkin," said the skeleton, whose name was Edgar. "I'm afraid my foot fell off again —I had to scramble around to find it among all your shoes. You know, it wouldn't hurt you to clean up in there once in a while."

"I was asleep," said Herbert the monster, yawning and scratching himself somewhere unpleasant.

"I couldn't get the window open!" screeched the ghost, who was named Arthur. "You try opening a window when you keep going *through* everything! It's not as easy as it looks being me!"

"Then why didn't you just go *through the window* to get in?" said Edgar.

"Oh, so you're an expert on ghosts now, are you, Mr. Limbs-keep-falling-off?" said Arthur, whizzing around the room like a dizzy fly.

"Don't use that tone with me, you pointless puff of smoke," snapped Edgar, shaking a bony finger. "I was just stating the obvious. I mean, how long have you been a ghost? Five years? You'd think you'd have at least mastered the basics by now."

"Maybe if you didn't put me down all the time, I'd have the courage to fly through something!" yelled Arthur.

"Oh, for goodness' sake—so now it's *my* fault that you're the afterlife's greatest underachiever?" Edgar cracked.

"Stop it!" cried Dinkin. "We don't have time for this!"

"Do we have time for breakfast? I'm hungry," said Herbert.

"No, we don't have time for breakfast! And anyway it's the middle of the . . . Look, we're getting sidetracked! The fact is, we're all in serious danger!" said Dinkin.

"What's happened?" said Arthur.

"The worst, most terrifying, most horrendous thing in the world has happened!" said Dinkin. "That's what!"

"What is it?" cried Edgar, his bones rattling. "More bears? Tell me it's not more bears . . ."

"Worse . . . ," said Dinkin, leaning toward the light. "It's the *girl next door*."

"AAAAAHHH!" screamed Arthur. "Let's get out of here!" He grabbed hold of Dinkin, turning him ghostly, and started zooming around the room with him, flying through the bed, through the walls, even through Herbert and Edgar!

"Put me down! You know I hate it when you make me all ghostly," said Dinkin. "And I haven't even told you why she's terrifying yet!"

"You mean, it's worse than the fact that she's a *girl*?" said Arthur, releasing Dinkin so he dropped to the floor with a *SPLUD*!

"It's *much* worse," said Dinkin, picking himself up and rubbing his head. "I only got a quick look at her, and she was pretty far away . . . but as sure as peas are actually bedbugs rolled into a ball and painted green, the girl next door is not even *human*!"

"You mean . . . ?" said Arthur.

"Worse," said Dinkin.

"You . . . you can't possibly mean . . . ," said Edgar, gnawing at his bony knuckles.

"Worse," said Dinkin.

"Not . . . not . . . not . . . ," began Herbert. Then after a moment he said, "Wait, I've forgotten what we were talking about . . ."

"I knew it from the first moment I saw

her," said Dinkin. "The blank staring eyes, the bloodthirsty expression, the pigtails . . . it was so obvious! The girl next door is a *flesh-eating alien space zombie from beyond horror*!"

"AAAAAHHHHAHHH!" screamed The Frightening Things, who were usually even more scared of absolutely everything than Dinkin. Still, they were always willing to help, and that meant Dinkin never had to face his fears alone.

"That's *still* not even the most terrifying part," sighed Dinkin. "'Cause if I know my flesh-eating alien space zombies from beyond horror as well as I think I do, she's planning on turning the whole planet into mindless, flesh-eating slaves!"

"But what on earth can we do?" said Edgar, his bones rattling with fear.

"We do what we always do," said Dinkin. *"Panic!"*

THE TROUBLE WITH FLESH-EATING ALIEN SPACE ZOMBIES FROM BEYOND HORROR

Time spent working on The Plan Not to Get Eaten by the Flesh-Eating Alien Space Zombie from Beyond Horror or Even Worse, Get Turned into a Flesh-Eating Zombie by the Flesh-Eating Alien Space Zombie from Beyond Horror: 5 hours 14 minutes

28

Dinkin and The Frightening Things stayed up all night working on The Plan Not to Get Eaten by the Flesh-Eating Alien Space Zombie From Beyond Horror or Even Worse, Get Turned into a Flesh-Eating Zombie by the Flesh-Eating Alien Space Zombie from Beyond Horror (which they ended up just calling "The Plan"). Dinkin got out some pens and a large piece of paper and wrote down everything they knew about flesh-eating alien space zombies from beyond horror ("zombaliens" for short). The five things everyone agreed on were:

1. Zombaliens spend all their time trying to conquer the universe by turning everyone into zombies, except on Sundays, when they watch all the TV they missed while they were busy turning everyone into zombies.

2. Zombaliens wear human disguises to blend in so that they can zombify in secret and go shopping and stuff.

3. Zombaliens use lemon juice and furniture polish to cover up their natural smell, which is a cross between sour milk and old ladies' underwear.

4. Zombaliens do not celebrate Christmas.

5. Zombaliens have no weaknesses (or if they do, they've kept them really quiet).

On the other side of the piece of paper, they wrote down the best ways of dealing with a zombalien encounter. So far they only had . . .

. . . neither of which seemed to be very good solutions.

Weak spot

"We need proof that the girl is a zombalien, and we need it fast. Otherwise, we'll all be zombified before we even get to the weekend," said Dinkin, marking the potential weak spots

Weak spot

(ankles, ears, pigtails) on a drawing of a zombalien.

"I can't be zombified this weekend, I've got things to do," said Arthur, nervously checking his diary.

Weak spot

"I'm not sure the zombalien next door is going to put off her conquest of the world so you can go and play World of Poltergeists on your Hex-Box," Edgar spat.

"Well, exc-u-use me for having a hobby!" said Arthur, flying in and out of Dinkin's pants drawer for no good reason.

"Stop it, you two, this is getting us nowhere," said Dinkin. "Herbert, any ideas?"

The Frightening Things looked at Herbert. He had eaten most of Dinkin's pens. He burped loudly and sprayed colored ink all over the wall.

"Pardon me," he said.

"As I was *saying*," continued a frustrated Dinkin, "we need to find a way to —"

"Too late . . . ," said Edgar. He pointed out the window.

Far away, on the horizon, they could see the sun rising.

"AAA-A-AAH!" said Arthur. "We lost track of time! Here comes the sun!"

"But you can't go yet, we don't have a plan!" said Dinkin.

"You know as well as we do that we can only come out at night," said Edgar. "We are Frightening Things, after all."

"Fine, but don't blame me if I'm a zombie the next time I see you," said Dinkin.

"Call for us at midnight . . . ," said Edgar as he began to fade. And with that, The Frightening Things disappeared. Dinkin was alone again. He sighed and yawned at the same time, wondering how his zombalien-filled day could get any worse. Four seconds later, there was a knock on Dinkin's door. It was his mother.

"Morning, Dinkin, up already? Oh, good! That gives you plenty of time to get ready for school . . ."

HARD TO BELIEVE

Time: 5:34 AM
Time until school bell: 3 hours,
11 minutes
Time until global zombification: ?

"School? SCHOOL? I can't go to school!
There's a *zombalien* on the loose!" cried
Dinkin, peeking through the curtains. Now,
normally, Dinkin didn't bother telling his
parents about his most terrifying fears.
They tended to just say, "Oh, don't be so
ridiculous," or "Here we go again," which
was obviously frustrating when Dinkin was
being menaced by, for example, heat-seeking
bananas or man-eating bicycles. At least The
Frightening Things understood him. They
were usually all he needed to get things back

to acceptable levels of scariness. But this time things were different—the whole world was in danger from the zombalien. He had to try and make his mom understand.

"I'm sorry, a zom-ba-what?" said Mrs. Dings.

"A zombalien! A flesh-eating alien space zombie from beyond horror!" yelled Dinkin.

"Oh, Dinkin, don't be so silly," said Mrs. Dings.

"I knew you'd say that! It's just like the bears! And the mind-control toothpaste! And the exploding dinner ladies, and the dinosaur-making machine, and the killer clouds! You never believe me!" cried Dinkin.

"It's not that we don't believe you . . . it's just that sometimes you're hard to believe," said Mrs. Dings. "And it's *so* early for flesh-feeding zomb-a-whatsits from wherever. Now *please* get ready for school like a good boy."

"But the girl next door is going to turn me

into a mindless slave!" cried Dinkin.

"Well, that would certainly make my life easier," sighed Dinkin's mom. "You never know, using your mind just a little less might mean you don't *worry* so much about everything. Now go to school—and *no arguments*."

As she ushered Dinkin into the bathroom to wash up, she spotted a couple of half-eaten magic markers on the floor.

"Have . . . have you been *eating* pens?" she asked.

"That wasn't me, it was—," began Dinkin.

"Don't tell me," said Mrs. Dings, in the sort of voice grown-ups use when they think you're lying. "It was The Frightening Things . . . "

TO SCHOOL
AND BACK

Length of bus ride to school: 720
seconds
Length of school day: 23,400
seconds
Length of longest thirteen
seconds ever recorded: 168
seconds

36   It had just turned 8:06 when the school
bus arrived. Dinkin was rushing around
the house collecting "equipment" to protect
himself against a zombalien attack when his
mother grabbed him and manhandled him
out of the house.

"Wait! I don't have everything I
need! What if she's at school, too? I'll be
defenseless! I haven't even field-tested my
Zombalien-Tracking Wrist Radar!" protested
Dinkin.

"Dinkin, I don't think the girl next

door has started at your school yet," said Mrs. Dings as she ushered him onto the bus.

"What? How do you know?" asked Dinkin.

"Well, because she's over there— look," said Mrs. Dings. Dinkin looked over to the house next door. There, standing on the lawn of next-door's garden, was the zombalien. She was playing with a small, brown dog and making it do tricks.

"Mom, run! Run for your life!" shouted Dinkin as the bus doors closed, but she didn't seem to hear him. As the bus set off, he rushed to an empty seat and stared helplessly through the window as his mother waved him off.

Typical, thought Dinkin. *Now I'll get home and find my mom drooling slime on the floor and saying things like "Eat brains!" and "Graaagh!"*

The ride to school seemed to take forever, but once he was there, Dinkin was so worried about his mom being zombified that he completely failed to notice these four extremely terrifying things:

8:48 am: Dinkin's teacher, Ms. Feebleback, accidentally misses Dinkin on the attendance sheet. (Which, according to Dinkin, only happens when you suddenly cease to exist.)

10:12 am: A butterfly flies into the classroom during a video on personal safety. (Which Dinkin would normally take as a signal of an all-out butterfly invasion.)

12:33 pm: Dinkin is served carrots by the lunch lady, Mrs. Hogjaw. (Dinkin doesn't eat carrots because they are the noses of snowmen, and Dinkin doesn't like the idea of eating anybody's nose.)

3:03 pm: Boris Wack, the biggest boy in class 9D, tells Dinkin he smells. (Last time this happened, Dinkin sewed three hundred car air fresheners onto his school uniform. The school was closed for the rest of the week due to what the principal called "Pine Pollution.")

In fact, the whole day passed in a blur of zombalien-related anxiety. Before Dinkin knew it, he was back on the bus, chugging toward home and who-knows-what kinds of horrors. The bus dropped Dinkin off just before the zombalien's house. It was eerily silent. *Maybe she's zombified the whole street already!* thought Dinkin.

He crept past the house as quietly as he could, but before long, the thought of being zombified from behind was too scary to bear. He began skipping, then jogging, then running, and finally sprinting for his life. He reached his house and banged on the door, praying that his mother had not become a mindless, brain-sucking pawn in the zombalien's evil scheme.

"Please not zombie, please not zombie . . . ," whispered Dinkin to himself. He took out a hastily constructed anti-zombalien grenade (which was pretty much just an egg with the words "anti-zombalien grenade" written on it. At least it hadn't broken in his bag, like the other five "grenades". . .). He waited for the longest thirteen seconds ever recorded. Finally, the door swung open and his mother appeared, not looking at all zombie-like.

"Hello, Dink," said Mrs. Dings.

"Mom, you're . . . you're okay!" said Dinkin.

"Of course I'm okay. Why wouldn't I be?"

"How are you feeling? Have you been bitten? Are you showing signs of zombieness? Do you have a craving to eat brains?" said Dinkin, without taking a breath.

"Oh, Dinkin, you're not still going on about Molly, are you? Honestly, you haven't even *met* her yet," said Mrs. Dings.

"Molly? Who's Molly? You mean the *zombalien*?" said Dinkin, panicking.

"I mean Molly, the girl next door. Now stop being such a nervous Nellie and come and say hello—she can't wait to meet you!" said Mrs. Dings.

Mrs. Dings stood aside. There, in the hallway, was Dinkin's worst nightmare, pigtails and all.

"Hi, Dinkin, I'm Molly. Do you want to play 'ponies'?"

MOLLY CODDLE (THE ZOMBALIEN NEXT DOOR)

Human count: 4
Canine count: 1
Flesh-Eating Alien Space Zombie
from Beyond Horror count: 1

One of the many problems Dinkin has with his mom is that she's nice to *everyone*, from old people to animals to total strangers. But inviting a zombalien into your *house*? That's like asking to have your brains eaten!

"Well, don't just stand there, come in and say hello to Molly," said Mrs. Dings, pulling Dinkin inside and bringing him face-to-face with the zombalien.

Dinkin froze.

"I like dolls and boy bands and combing my hair and my doggy, Princess Puppy-

Face, but mostly I like ponies! I'm '100% Pony Crazy', it says so on my T-shirt, look!" said Molly.

That's exactly what a zombalien pretending to be a human girl would say, thought Dinkin. Every instinct told him to run, but he knew that would give him away—the zombalien would realize that he knew her secret . . . and that would put him right at the top of her zombification list! He slipped the anti-zombalien grenade back into his pants pocket.

"You see? I knew you'd get along. Now, come and say hello to Mr. and Mrs. Coddle," said Mrs. Dings.

Dinkin could barely breathe as Molly skipped past him. Mrs. Dings nudged him into the living room, where he found Mr. and Mrs. Coddle snacking on some fancy cookies. They were both ridiculously smiley. Mr. Coddle looked like Santa Claus (but with brown hair and without the beard), and Mrs. Coddle looked like a crossing guard on her day off. At Mrs. Coddle's feet sat the small, brown dog, who immediately started barking when Dinkin entered the room.

"AAAH!" screamed Dinkin, who was terrified of all animal noises. Even the sound of a cat purring gave him a nervous rash.

"Oh, don't worry about Princess Puppy-Face, she's just grumpy because she hasn't had her lunch," said Mrs. Coddle. "Hello to you, young man—you must be Duncan."

"*Dinkin*," whimpered a petrified Dinkin.

"Pleased to meet you, Duncan," said Mr. Coddle.

"*Dinkin*," said Dinkin.

"Duncan?" said Mr. Coddle.

"Dinkin," said Mrs. Dings.

"Dinkin?" said Mrs. Coddle.

"Duncan," said Dinkin. "No wait, Dinkin!"

"Dinkin is a funny name," said Molly, playing with her pigtails.

"Maybe on your planet," muttered Dinkin.

"What?" said Molly.

"Nothing," said Dinkin.

"Well, Duncan, I can't tell you how

excited we are about Molly having someone to play with," said Mr. Coddle.

Dinkin dabbed the sweat from his forehead. How could they not see that their own daughter was an undead creature from another planet? How long had this been going on? Had she been "replaced" recently? One thing was certain—only he had seen through the zombalien's disguise.

"Dinkin, why don't you and Molly go and play in the garden?" said Mrs. Dings.

"What? No! I mean, I can't! Don't make me!" said Dinkin, holding on to his mom for dear life.

"Don't worry, Duncan, Molly doesn't *bite*," said Mr. Coddle. This was too much for Dinkin to take. He ran screaming out of the living room and up the stairs.

"Yay! Kiss chase!" giggled Molly, and she ran after him.

ESCAPE ROUTE
SEVEN-ZERO-SEVEN

Cloud cover: 14%
Comet threat: 2.2%
Need for escape route: 100%

48 Dinkin dashed into his bedroom and slammed the door. He could hear Molly behind him, giggling with bloodthirsty glee. There, in the corner of the room, was the Fortress of Ultimate Protection. Dinkin dived in and closed the Drawbridge of Absolutely-No-Entry-Whatsoever-Ness. He was halfway through activating the Force Field of Just-To-Be-On-The-Safe-Side-Ness when the roof of the fortress was lifted off.

"Found you!" said Molly. She had somehow managed to get past security!

Dinkin scrambled through the Secret Getaway Tunnel of You-Never-Know-When-You'll-Need-a-Secret-Getaway-Tunnel-Even-in-a-Fortress-of-Ultimate-Protection-Ness, which brought him out at the foot of his bed.

"Kissy, kissy!" squealed Molly as she blocked the bedroom door. She puckered her lips as if she was about to bite his head off.

"Stay away!" screamed Dinkin as Molly ran toward him. *If only it was midnight*, he thought. *If it was midnight, The Frightening Things could save me! Or at least distract the zombalien with their terrified screams. But now, there's no way out! NO WAY OUT!*

Then he remembered *Escape Route SEVEN-ZERO-SEVEN*. Because Dinkin expected that danger lay around every corner, he had figured out ways to escape from every room he'd ever been in—from the kitchen, from his classroom, even from his Aunt Hattie's weird underground bathroom. He had worked out over a thousand escape routes, but the seven hundred seventh was a particular favorite.

Dinkin reached for the window. He unhooked the latch and it swung open.

"What are you doing?" asked Molly as Dinkin climbed onto the window ledge.

"Looks like you're going to go hungry, zombalien!" cried Dinkin . . .

. . . and then he leaped out the window!

THE NOT-QUITE DEATH OF DINKIN DINGS

Pollen count: 35 (moderate)
Not-Quite Death count: 1 (so far)

"Mommy! Daddy!" screamed Molly as she raced downstairs. "Dinkin's dead!"

"What?!" cried Mrs. Dings.

"Duncan's *dead*? How?" said Mr. Coddle.

"He jumped out the window!"

"Oh, my! *Dinkin*!" said Mrs. Dings. Everyone ran out of the house into the front garden. Dinkin's bedroom window was open, but there was no sign of him. Mrs. Dings ran around the garden frantically calling out "Dinkin! Dinkin!" She searched behind the tree, in the hammock, even in

the bed of
nearly award-
winning begonias. Then, all of a
sudden, she stopped in her tracks.
It was as if she'd just remembered
something.

"Wait a minute . . . did Dinkin jump
out his *bedroom* window? The one by
the tree?" asked Mrs. Dings. She pointed
to the old oak tree that stood on the
front lawn.

Molly nodded. Mrs. Dings looked at
the window, then at the old oak tree.

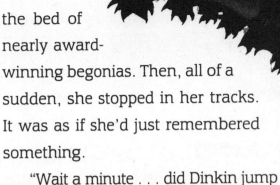

She saw a long, thick
rope dangling from a
high branch. It was just
long enough to reach Dinkin's
window.

"Not Escape Route SEVEN-
ZERO-SEVEN *again* . . . Dinkin!
Come down from there this
minute!"

Sure enough, there, perched in the tree, was Dinkin. He was gripping the trunk of the tree with one hand, but with the other, he held what looked very much like an egg.

"Hey, zombalien! Eat anti-zombalien grenade!" he yelled.

"*Dinkin Danger Dings*, don't you dare throw that!" shouted Mrs. Dings in a surprisingly stern voice.*

*(Yes, Danger really *was* Dinkin's middle name. Who would have guessed?)

But it was too late. Dinkin threw the grenade right at Molly!

Well, he meant to. In fact, the grenade missed Molly by a good foot or so, and landed— *SPLAT!*—right in Mrs. Coddle's face.

54

"AAAH!" yelled Mrs. Coddle.

"Dinkin!" screamed Mrs. Dings.

"Mom, run! That was my only grenade!" said Dinkin. He began to climb higher up the tree. He would have reached the top, too, if he hadn't spotted his dad, driving home from work. He screamed and waved both his arms . . .

"*Dad*! Turn back!"

. . . And then fell out of the tree.

THU-
DUMP!

THREE MINUTES
LATER

Time taken for Dinkin to come
to: 3 minutes
Time needed for Mrs. Coddle to
clean egg out of hair: 18 minutes
Time needed for Molly Coddle to
zombify whole street: 1.6 days

56 When Dinkin came to, his parents' faces
loomed over him.

"Are you all right, Dink?" said Mr. Dings.

"Wh-what happened?" said Dinkin,
rubbing his head.

"You fell out of the oak tree again,
Dinkin. And knocked yourself out, *again*.
How many times is that? Eight?" said
Mr. Dings.

"*Nine*," said Mrs. Dings.

"You see, this is what I don't understand,"
continued Mr. Dings, taking off his glasses

and wiping them with a cloth. "You're too scared to wear socks, you have nightmares about sliced bread, and you can't even look at a *picture* of a kitten. Yet you'll happily throw yourself out of an upstairs window! It doesn't make sense!"

"Well, wouldn't *you* rather jump out of a window than be forever transformed into the mindless slave of a flesh-eating alien space zombie from beyond horror?" said Dinkin as if he were stating the ridiculously obvious.

"Well, you can't argue with that, I suppose," sighed Mr. Dings. "What is this zombo-thingy business, anyway?"

"Don't get him started, dear," said Mrs. Dings. "He's been going on about Molly being a zomb-a-whatsit all day."

"A zombalien! Zom-bay-lee-un! It's really not hard to remember!" cried Dinkin. Suddenly his eyes grew wide with horror. "Where *is* the zombalien? Is she still here? Is she waiting for me?"

"If you mean Molly, she and her parents have gone home. And they're not at all happy," said Mrs. Dings. "You just can't go around throwing eggs at people, Dinkin."

"I don't feel zombified . . . did she bite me?" said Dinkin, panicking.

"Did who bite you? You mean Princess Puppy-Face?" said Mrs. Dings.

"No, *Molly*!" said Dinkin.

"Of course not! Honestly, Dinkin, you're not making any sense," said Mrs. Dings.

"Maybe we should take him to the doctor's, just to be sure. He has a nasty bump on the head," said Mr. Dings.

"The doctor's?" squealed Dinkin. "No, not the doctor's, anything but that!"

As far as Dinkin was concerned, going to the doctor's didn't make you better—it was just an easy way to catch some horrible disease. The doctor's waiting room was, after all, *full of sick people*. Every time he went, he was sure he had caught something terrible.

Only this year he had complained of:

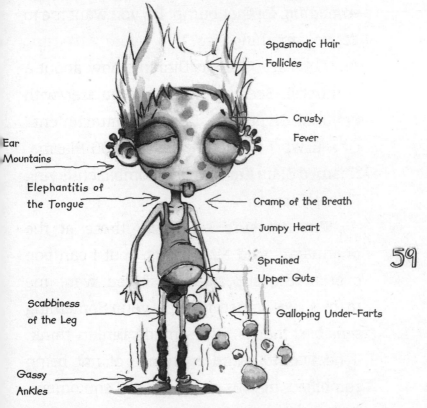

Spasmodic Hair Follicles

Crusty Fever

Ear Mountains

Elephantitis of the Tongue

Cramp of the Breath

Jumpy Heart

Sprained Upper Guts

Scabbiness of the Leg

Galloping Under-Farts

Gassy Ankles

"Please, I don't need to go to the doctor's! I feel fine! Better than fine!" said Dinkin. He tapped the bump on his head and stifled a scream. "See? I feel great!"

"All right, all right," said Mrs. Dings.

"But I'll need to go to the pharmacy and get something for that bump. Do you want me to get you anything else?"

"Let's see," began Dinkin, "how about a Zombalien-Seeking M3000 Megalaser with optional Hypervolt Bazooka attachment? Or a Class 7 Battletank with T-400 Plasma-Charged Slam Cannon and Zombalien-Frying Flame-Thrower?"

"I'm not sure I can get those at the pharmacy," said Mrs. Dings, "but I can pop over to the supermarket if you want me to pick up something for you. Something *sensible*, that is." This made Dinkin think. If he was to stand a chance of not being zombified, he was going to need equipment. Tools to help reveal Molly's secret to the world and rid her from his life forever.

But that meant going somewhere he swore he'd never go again. And saying something he never thought he'd say:

"Can I come to the supermarket, too?"

THE CHAPTER WHERE DINKIN BRAVES THE SUPERMARKET

Stranger danger: 12.46%
Sky-falling-in danger: 33.09%
Supermarket danger: 111.11%

Despite their suspicions, Mr. and Mrs. Dings agreed to take Dinkin with them to the supermarket. Dinkin *hated* the supermarket. It had to be the most dangerous place in the world! There were a trillion and one hidden hazards that *no one* warned you about: loose-wheeled shopping carts that went in every direction but forward; vegetables covered in dirt and dirty pesticides; jars of pasta sauce just waiting to leap off the shelf and shatter into a half-sharp, half-slippery slide of death . . . the list was endless!

In fact, the only thing Dinkin hated more than the supermarket was facing a zombalien unprepared. He held on to his dad as he walked around the aisles looking for good anti-zombalien equipment.

This is what he picked up:

2 meat-tenderizing mallets with rubber handles: $8.99

I DVD of *Revenge of the Sweaty Undead From Planet Fear: The Musical*: $14.97

2 large bags of barbecue charcoal: $9.99

3 cans of lighter fluid: $10.47

I cordless power drill: $99.99

36 large, free-range eggs: $8.94

His dad, of course, made him put all of those things back.

Then he picked up . . .

I waterproof, disposable camera with flash: $3.99

I packet of bacon: $1.99

and

I super-squeaky dog chew toy (bone shaped): $0.98

. . . which he was allowed to keep.

"What do you want this stuff for,

anyway?" asked Mrs. Dings at the checkout. "I hope this has nothing to do with poor Molly Coddle."

"*Poor* Molly Coddle? You mean, *poor* Molly Coddle the bloodsucking undead creature from another galaxy?" cried Dinkin in frustration.

"Someone's being silly again," laughed Mr. Dings.

"Seriously silly," added Mrs. Dings.

"*Stupendously* silly!" said Mr. Dings.

Dinkin's parents continued to find ways of describing how silly it was to think Molly Coddle was a zombalien.

By the time they left the supermarket, Dinkin was sillier than seventeen silly sailors. By the time they got home, they had named him "General Dinkin the Silly, who sailed a schooner filled with six hundred silly sailors along the seven seas."

But Dinkin knew it was his parents' own silliness that was going to get them both zombified if they didn't start taking him seriously. Now more than ever, he needed proof.

DOG DAY AFTERNOON

Fear of outdoors: 17%
Fear of dogs: 53%
Fear of zombaliens: 97%

66 Dinkin knew that every second wasted was a second closer to zombification. The Frightening Things wouldn't reappear for another seven hours, but Dinkin had to act *now*. He shut himself in his bedroom and got to work on his Zomb-O-Tron 6000. He made a helmet out of a colander and one of his dad's best shirts, added the camera and a small pen-flashlight, then wrapped around some radiation-reflecting tinfoil and attached a small mirror using glue and spit. Finally, he taped a plunger to the front.

By the time afternoon turned into early evening, the Zomb-O-Tron 6000 was complete. It may well have been Dinkin's fifth greatest creation—much better than the Zomb-O-Tron 5000! The secret was in the head-mounted Mask-Demasker. All he needed to do was stick the sucker to Molly's disguise and yank it off! He'd have a clear shot of her in all her zombalien hideousness! One click of the camera and he'd have the evidence he needed. He just had to get close enough to use it.

Dinkin secured the Zomb-O-Tron 6000 to his head and peered out his bedroom window into the garden next door.

At first he didn't see it, then he caught a flash of pigtail. There she was—Molly the zombalien—playing with Princess Puppy-Face in the front garden.

"Got to get closer," whispered Dinkin. Fortunately, he had the perfect invention for such a challenge. He ran downstairs and out the back door. There, at the side of the patio, sat a large, black trash can with wheels. Dinkin took it by the handle and steered it around to the front of the house. He was almost there when his mother blocked his path.

"I thought you were scared of trash cans," she said suspiciously.

"I *am*," said Dinkin. Then he looked at the trash can. "Oh, you mean this? This isn't a trash can. It may look like one, but then that's the whole point of . . . the Concealinator."

The Concealinator was one of Dinkin's earliest and best inventions. He often used it to hide from (and spy on) anyone who came to the house. With a few simple changes, he had created the perfect mobile shelter. Though it looked like a normal trash can, the Concealinator was as tough as a tank. At least that's what Dinkin hoped.

"Well, whatever you're up to, *try* and stay out of trouble." Mrs. Dings sighed and went back into the house.

"Okay, Agent Dings, time to go behind enemy lines," whispered Dinkin to himself, hyperventilating with fear. He lifted the lid, took out the trash bags, and got in (being careful not to trap his plunger).

Then, from the inside, he detached the false bottom, put his feet through the holes he'd cut out of the real bottom, and flipped open the viewing window. The Concealinator was complete! Although perfectly disguised, Dinkin could see where he was going and propel himself along! He shuffled the Concealinator around to the front of the house.

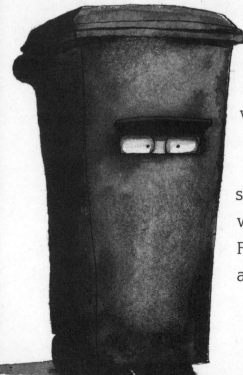

"Target sighted— approach w-with c-caution," he stuttered, breathless with horror.

Sure enough, there was Molly, still happily playing with Princess Puppy-Face. She was too far away for a clear shot. Slowly, carefully,

Dinkin edged the Concealinator toward them. Within thirty-six seconds, he was at close range. And she didn't suspect a thing!

"Target unaware—proximity achieved," whispered Dinkin to himself. He inched his head up, opening the trash can lid just a crack, and stuck out the Zomb-O-Tron 6000's Mask-Demasker. All he needed to do was attach the sucker to her head and *bingo*—no more mask! He was only feet away from revealing her secret! Suddenly he saw Princess Puppy-Face's ears prick up.

"What is it, Princess?" said Molly. Princess Puppy-Face gave a low growl and started barking at the Concealinator!

Arf! Arf! Arf!

Then she began to race toward him. Dinkin was gripped with horror—he was nearly as scared of dogs as he was of zombaliens! He closed his eyes and hoped that the earth would open up and swallow him.

"What are you barking at? It's just a stupid trash can . . . ," said Molly. Finally, after what seemed like 19.6 seconds, the yapping stopped. There was silence. Dinkin sighed with relief. Maybe the disguise had worked . . . he *did* look like a bin, after all! He dared to open an eye and peer out of the window. For a moment he wasn't sure what he was seeing. Then he realized: It was *Molly's* face.

"Hi, Dinkin! What are you doing in there?" said Molly.

"AAAAAA-AAAHAAHHHH!" screamed Dinkin. The zombalien had found him! He spun the Concealinator around and headed back toward the house as fast as he could.

"Can I play, too?" shouted Molly. She ran after him, closely followed by a barking Princess Puppy-Face.

"AAAA-AAHAH!" screamed Dinkin again, plowing the Concealinator straight into a tree and throwing himself onto the front lawn.

"Hee-hee! You fell down!" squealed Molly, running toward him.

"Mom! Dad! *Help*!" screamed Dinkin, scrambling along the ground.

"*ARF! ARF!*" yapped Princess Puppy-Face.

"You're funny, Dinkin!" cried Molly.

"Get away from me! I don't want to be a zombie!" screamed Dinkin, but it was too late. Molly loomed over him. Dinkin closed his eyes and prepared for the worst, when . . .

"What's going on out here? It's past your bedtime, Molly Coddle!"

Dinkin turned slowly to see who it was. There, on the lawn, stood Mr. and Mrs. Coddle.

"Molly, I thought we told you to get your pajamas on," said Mr. Coddle.

"I was playing with Dinkin," said Molly, twisting a pigtail.

"It's too late for playing," said Mrs. Coddle. "Duncan's older than you—he doesn't have to go to bed yet. But you should have been tucked in ages ago!"

"*ARF! ARF!*" yapped Princess Puppy-Face.

"That's enough from you, Princess," said Mr. Coddle. As Princess Puppy-Face scampered off, Mr. and Mrs. Coddle took Molly by the hand and led her indoors. Dinkin tried to call out "Don't go in there! She's a zombalien! You're in severe danger!" but he was paralyzed with fear.

Molly looked back at Dinkin and grinned. "See you in the morning!" she shouted.

In the morning? thought Dinkin.

Then she's planning on zombifying me first thing tomorrow! He only had one night to reveal her secret to the world! And one thing was certain . . .

. . . he couldn't do it alone . . .

THE RETURN OF THE FRIGHTENING THINGS

Chance of rain: 94%
Chance of making it through
the night: 3%

76 Dinkin lay awake in bed. Now more than
ever, he needed the help of The Frightening
Things.

He watched as the clock ticked
from 11:59 PM to the much more useful
12:00 AM. Dinkin took the Ancient
Summoning Parchment from under the
Ancient Summoning Mattress and assumed
the Ancient Summoning Position (a cross
between kneeling and pooing). Then (at
12:00:22) he took a deep summoning breath
and began:

"*Frightening Things, Frightening Things*
Creep from the gloom,
Crawl from the shadows and into my room,
Frightening Things, Frightening Things
Come to my aid,
Save me from danger (and being afraid!)."

Dinkin waited for the Frightening Things to appear. (12:01:04)

And then waited a bit longer. (12:01:59)

Nothing. (12:02:16)

Not so much as a whiff of ghostly wind. (12:02:26)

Where were they? (12:02:34) Dinkin's heart skipped several beats. What if they'd disappeared, never to return? (12:02:45) What if they'd got lost in . . . wherever it was that they went during the day? What if they'd gotten bored? Or worse, what if they'd gotten sick of being at the beck and call of a nine-and-a-quarter-year-old boy? (12:02:56) It was all too much to bear. Dinkin repeated the chant:

"FRIGHTENING-THINGS-FRIGHTENING-THINGS-CREEP-FROM-THE-GLOOM-CRAWL-FROM-THE-SHA—"

The closet burst open! Edgar the skeleton tumbled out, and immediately began jabbering wildly. Unfortunately, he had lost his bottom jaw, so he could only speak in vowels:

"Ih-ih, I oh o-ee I ay, I ih oo-ih or eye aw aw ay, uh I arr eye ih eh-ee-air! A oo ee ih?"

[*Translated for the benefit of those who don't speak Vowel: "Dinkin, I'm so sorry I'm late, I've been looking for my jaw all day, but I can't find it anywhere! Have you seen it?"*]

A moment later, Herbert crawled out from under the bed. He had his mouth crammed full.

"Dorry I bade, Dib-gib. I wud jud abib a bid-eye dack," he said.

[*Translation for the benefit of those who don't speak Talking With Your Mouth Full: "Sorry I'm late, Dinkin. I was just having a midnight snack."*]

"What's going on?" huffed Dinkin. "Can't I leave you alone for nineteen-and-a-half hours without you all losing your voices?"

"Mm? Oh, dorry," said Herbert, and took something large and yellow out of his mouth. It was Edgar's jaw! Edgar screamed in rage and pounced on Herbert, sending them both crashing into the wall!

"Oo at oh, a eye aw, o-h or ih-er!" said Edgar, his bony fingers wrapped around Herbert's neck.

[*Translation: "You fat oaf, that's my jaw, not your dinner!"*]

"It's not my fault, I'm a monster-under-the-bed! Eating stuff I find lying around is in my nature!" said Herbert, struggling to get free.

As Edgar and Herbert tumbled around the room, Arthur flew through the window.

"Sorry I'm late, I've been dodging raindrops all the way here . . . It's going to be a stormy night, I can feel it in my vapors! So, what did I miss?" he said, and immediately got caught up in the tumbling mass of bones, scales, and slobber.

"Stop it! STOP IT" cried Dinkin, throwing the blanket on top of The Frightening Things to try and put a stop to their fighting. "We've got bigger things to worry about!"

It was at that moment that Dinkin's dad stuck his head in the room.

"What's going on, Dink?" said Mr. Dings. "You do know it's the middle of the night . . ."

"It's not me, it's The Frightening Things—they're messing around," said Dinkin.

Mr. Dings looked at the blanket on the floor. It seemed to have something underneath it. *Probably a pile of clothes*, he thought. Still, he knew better than to debate the existence of The Frightening Things—it was better that Dinkin had three imaginary friends than no friends at all.

"Well, just try to get some sleep, okay? And maybe turn the volume down a bit," said Mr. Dings.

"Don't tell me, tell them!" said Dinkin.

Mr. Dings stared at the blanket.

"Um . . . right. You guys keep it down as well," he said.

And with a shake of his head, Mr. Dings closed the door and went back to bed.

Dinkin lifted up the blanket.

"Right, no more messing around. We've got one night to blow that zombalien's cover —or I'm *doomed*," he said.

"Eye oh ee . . . ?" began Edgar, then managed to put his jaw back in. "That's better—I mean, why, what's happened?"

"What's happened? You mean, besides being chased around the house by a hungry zombalien, knocked unconscious, barked at by a dog that clearly has a grudge against me, and nearly turned into a *zombie*?" screeched Dinkin. "Well, *besides* that, the *worst* thing in the *world* has happened! The zombalien knows I know she's a zombalien! And she knows I know she knows I know!"

The Frightening Things looked a bit confused.

"Which *means* I'm going to be her first victim! She's going to zombify me tomorrow morning!"

"AAAAAAAAAHHHHHHH!!!"

screamed The Frightening Things.

"Our only chance is to reveal her secret tonight, before she gets a chance to transform me into a mindless, brain-sucking slave. We'll need our wits, my Zomb-O-Tron 6000, and this—the Dog-Distracter Mark IV," said Dinkin, holding up the chew toy he'd bought. It was wrapped in a piece of bacon and had a long piece of string attached to one end.

"What's that?" asked Herbert.

"*That* is the final part of *The Plan*," said Dinkin.

"Oh, so there is a plan this time?" said Edgar.

"Well, *sort of*," said Dinkin.

THE PLAN (AS OF 12:58 AM)

1) DINKIN AND THE FRIGHTENING THINGS make it to the CODDLE'S house without chickening out. (Likelihood of success: 52%)

    2) EDGAR and HERBERT (Super Secret Team ALPHA-1) distract PRINCESS PUPPY-FACE with the DOG-DISTRACTOR MARK IV. The coast is clear! (Likelihood of success: 39%)

    3) DINKIN and ARTHUR (Super Secret Team BETA-2) FLY into the house through the WINDOW. (Likelihood of success: 27%)

    4) DINKIN and ARTHUR locate the ZOMBALIEN using the ZOMB-O-TRON 6000, DEMASK the ZOMBALIEN, and PHOTOGRAPH it in all its HIDEOUSNESS! (Likelihood of success: 18%)

5) Having NOT been EATEN, ZOMBIFIED, or BARKED at, both teams then RETREAT to the relative safety of Dinkin's bedroom for debriefing and a GLASS OF MILK. (Likelihood of there being enough milk for everyone: 9%)

6) Dinkin shows the PICTURE OF THE ZOMBALIEN to the POLICE, the ARMY, the GOVERNMENT, and his PARENTS. The ZOMBALIEN'S secret is REVEALED TO THE WORLD! (Likelihood of success: 4%)

7) The zombalien FLEES back to the far reaches of SPACE! The world is SAVED from Dinkin's neighbor! (Likelihood of success: 0.4%)

[Please note that The Frightening Things' terrified objections to The Plan (all 93 of them) have been removed due to lack of space.]

THE CHAPTER WHERE DINKIN AND THE FRIGHTENING THINGS NEATLY EXECUTE THE PLAN

Chance of The Plan being neatly executed: 4.2%

"This isn't going to be easy," said Dinkin to The Frightening Things as the rain beat down on the window. The storm was going to make an impossible job even harder. "We have no idea what our enemy is capable of. There is more danger out there than we've ever faced before, and not just everyday stuff, like poisonous blackbirds or psycho-mice. There's a zombalien in that house, and I'm number one on her people-to-zombify-before-breakfast list. But as long as we work together, we can possibly, maybe, sort of, reveal her secret."

"We're with you, Dinkin!" shouted Arthur. "I mean, unless things get *really* scary . . . "

Dinkin put on the Zomb-O-Tron 6000 and handed Edgar the Dog-Distracter Mark IV. He saw Herbert lick his lips with both tongues.

"Don't eat it," said Dinkin. "That's for Princess Puppy-Face. And make sure you hold on to the string once she's taken the bait — we have to keep her in one place."

Dinkin and The Frightening Things snuck out of his room and made their way downstairs to the front door. By now the rain was falling harder than Dinkin had ever seen.

"I thought you didn't like rain, Dinkin," said Arthur.

Arthur was right. Of all weather-related horrors, Dinkin hated rain the most. After snow and sleet. And possibly fog. Anyway, he hated it. He thought it was like being in a shower for giants, but using only the cold faucets. And he was terrified of anything that involved giants. Or the cold. Or faucets.

"I'd rather be wet and alive than dry and a zombie," said Dinkin. He tucked his pajama bottoms into his rain boots, opened the door, and peered out. The rain fell in huge, angry drops and soaked the ground.

"Let's go," he said.

Dinkin Dings and The Frightening Things made their way slowly toward the Coddles' house. The freezing rain soaked Dinkin's pajamas and filled his boots. Edgar and Herbert huddled together as they

89

walked, their eyes darting around in dread. Arthur, who never got along well with water, was actually soaking up the raindrops.

"I'm filling up like a water balloon!" he moaned as he floated along.

"*Shhh!* We have to stay quiet!" whispered Dinkin. He was shaking so much with cold that he almost couldn't shake with fear. He stared up at the house, trying not to imagine the unimaginable horrors inside. As if on cue, a bolt of lightning lit up the sky. Dinkin and The Frightening Things covered their mouths all at once and tried not to scream!

"I'm not sure this is a good idea," squeaked Arthur. "I'm filling up! I can barely even float anymore!"

"We can't turn back now," said Dinkin,

trying to convince himself. "Super Secret Team ALPHA-1, deploy Dog-Distracter Mark IV."

"Hm? Oh, you mean us! Sorry, all this code-talk is baffling my bones . . . ," said Edgar. He and Herbert edged toward the front door, while Dinkin and Arthur ducked behind a hedge just in front of the house.

"Princess Puppy-Face? Are you in there?" whispered Edgar as he peered nervously through the mail slot. With no sign of her, he pushed the Dog-Distracter Mark IV through the gap and lowered it to the floor with the string. He waited for a moment, listening for the sound of Princess Puppy-Face's paw-steps.

"Is she taking it? Maybe she's asleep. Maybe she's not hungry. And if it's going to go to waste I could always take it off your hands . . . ," said Herbert, rubbing his belly.

"Shh! I hear her sniffing around . . . ," whispered Edgar. He held on tightly to the string, and pinned his ear cavity to the door.

CHOMP! The string tightened!

"She took it!" said Edgar. Sure enough, Princess Puppy-Face had sunk her teeth into the Dog-Distracter Mark IV. Edgar held on tight as she tugged on it. "I've got her! Dinkin — go!"

Suddenly, Edgar's arm was pulled through the mail slot, slamming him into the door with an enormous *SPWOK*!

"AAA-AH! She's got me! Herbert, help!" cried Edgar. Herbert grabbed him around the waist and pulled with all his monstrous might (which actually wasn't that much, as it turned out), but the more they struggled, the more Princess Puppy-Face fought back! Dinkin and Arthur looked on in horror from behind the hedge.

"We have to help—they're no match for one small dog!" said Arthur.

"We can't! We have to stick to The Plan!" said Dinkin, realizing with horror that that actually meant *carrying* out the rest of The Plan. He pinched himself and wiped the rain from his eyes. "W-we have to go, Arthur—fly us through that upstairs window."

"I'm not sure I can—I'm almost full of water!" said Arthur, trying to wring himself out like a wet dishcloth.

"It's too late to back out now — I'm going to be zombified in less than six hours!" said Dinkin frantically.

"All right, fine, but don't blame me if it's a bumpy ride," mumbled Arthur. He wrapped his arms around Dinkin, turning him ghostly, and carried him up into the air!

"Don't drop me!" squealed Dinkin as they floated slowly upward. He was, of course, terrified of heights. Although, being Dinkin, he was almost as afraid of going farther and farther up until he hit outer space as he was of falling.

Arthur did his best to dodge the raindrops, but it was no good. By the time they reached one of the upstairs windows he was almost completely waterlogged.

"Dinkin, I can't stay afloat, I'm too heavy!" cried Arthur.

"Hang on, we're almost there! Fly me through the window!" said Dinkin.

Arthur held his breath (or the ghostly equivalent). He flew at the window, hoping that he wasn't so full of water that they'd just splatter against it.

THE LAIR OF THE ZOMBALIEN

Chances of making it out alive: 2%
Chances of being turned into a
brain-eating zombie slave: 98%

96 Dinkin landed face-first on the hard floor.
It worked—he was inside!

"We did it, Arthur!" whispered Dinkin,
rubbing his nose. He looked around, but the
ghost was nowhere to be seen. Dinkin's eyes
scanned the room. "Arthur? Where are you?"

Dinkin looked out the window. There was
Arthur, still outside. He was so full of water
that (just as he'd feared) he'd splattered
against the window! He could barely even
stay in the air. As he started to sink out of
view, he mouthed, "Good luck."

Dinkin was alone in the house! And he wasn't even ghostly! Which meant that he was defenseless. Dinkin tried not to panic. Then, after panicking for two minutes and thirty-nine seconds, he tried again. He took several deep breaths and looked around. He could see:

A toilet.

A sink.

A towel with a picture of a pony on it.

He was in the Coddles' bathroom! This was it, there was no going back. Dinkin wiped the sweat from his brow, checked that the Zomb-O-Tron 6000 was still working, and tried to give himself a pep talk.

"Dinkin Danger Dings, you can do this. It's this or a lifetime of brain eating. Do you want to eat brains for the rest of your life? No. Are you sure? You don't sound sure. Of course I'm sure! Okay then, don't go on about it. I wasn't going on about it! Yes you were!"

After arguing with himself for another fifty-one seconds, Dinkin decided it was time to go. He opened the bathroom door and crept out into a moonlit corridor. Everything was silent. He turned on the Zomb-O-Tron 6000's flashlight, faintly illuminating two doors on his right, and another at the end.

Three doors to go.

The first door was shut tight. He reached out with a quivering hand and pulled it. It creaked open.

It was a *closet full of laundry*! "EemMph!!" Dinkin put his hand to his mouth to stop himself from screaming. Then he realized that he wasn't actually afraid of laundry, after all. He closed the door and moved on.

Two doors to go.

The second door was ajar. Dinkin slowly pushed it open. It was so dark he could barely see anything at all. Suddenly, there was a low, thunderous growl.

"EEeeepmMph!!" squeaked Dinkin, covering his mouth again. *That's not growling*, thought Dinkin. *That's snoring!* He was in Mr. and Mrs. Coddle's room! Dinkin backed silently out of the door, and continued down the corridor.

One door to go.

As he reached the door, he could see there was something written on it in big, pink letters:

Molly's Room
(come in and play)

He'd found it—the hideout of the zombalien! In his head, Dinkin was running home and hiding under the covers, but then he remembered that eating brains for the rest of his life was even *more* terrifying. He felt for the Zomb-O-Tron 6000, held his breath and (after another one minute and forty-two seconds of motionless dread) turned the door handle.

The zombalien's room was perfectly disguised as a human girl's room. It was *vile*. It was pink from floor to ceiling, and covered with boy-band posters and pictures of ponies and kittens. In the middle of the floor was a neatly laid out plastic tea set. In the corner of the room was a small bed. Dinkin took a step forward. It was empty!

"Where is she?" he whispered in panic.

Suddenly, the light came on, half-blinding Dinkin. He blinked nineteen times, until he could finally make out a shape in the doorway. It was Molly Coddle.

"Hello, Dinkin!" she said with glee. "Are you here for the tea party?"

TEA WITH MOLLY

Host: Molly Coddle
Invited guests: Miss Dolly,
Freddy Teddy
Uninvited guest: Dinkin
Danger Dings

Dinkin stared in frozen horror as Molly Coddle pretended to pour tea from her plastic teapot. She gave pretend tea to a doll and a cuddly bear before she got to Dinkin.

"Would you like sugar?" she asked.

"No, thank you very much, please," said Dinkin, so scared that he ended up sounding incredibly polite. Molly passed Dinkin a plastic teacup on a plastic saucer. There was a moment's silence. Why wasn't she in bed? More to the point, why wasn't she turning him into a zombie slave?

"I'm glad you came over for tea, even if it is the middle of the night, which is a little weird, but I don't mind," said Molly. "All my other friends are far away, where I used to live."

Yeah, far away in space, thought Dinkin, realizing that he had the perfect opportunity to reveal her secret. One good lunge with the Mask-Demasker and he could reveal her in all her hideousness! Of course, in The Plan, a) the zombalien was asleep and b) Dinkin was ghostly throughout. Dinkin shuddered with fear at the thought of having to do this without those two key ingredients.

"Where I used to live, far away, I had a

pony," said Molly, a little sadly. "She was called Polly. When we moved, I had to leave her behind. Now I don't have any friends and I don't have a pony." She put down her teacup and sniffled. Then she rubbed her eyes and wiped away a tear.

This is my chance . . . it's now or never! thought Dinkin. He aimed the Mask-Demasker at Molly, but as he edged toward her, Dinkin had a funny feeling. He stopped in his tracks, not quite believing what was happening. Despite himself, Dinkin was actually feeling a bit *sorry* for the zombalien.

"Sorry," said Molly, "I'm just a little bit sad."

Then a strange thing happened—Dinkin had a thought that he'd never had before in his whole life. What if he was wrong? What if maybe, just maybe, this sad little girl was actually *just* a sad little girl? He thought about all the things that had happened over the last two days. If Molly Coddle wasn't a flesh-eating alien space zombie from beyond horror, he had:

1) Run away from a little girl.

2) Thrown an egg at a little girl and accidentally hit a little girl's mom instead.

3) Gone to the supermarket. (And wasted six dollars and ninety-six cents.)

4) Gone outside in the middle of the night in the middle of a rainstorm.

Dinkin started to feel a little bit guilty. He also stopped worrying so much about being zombified.

"Do you like ponies?" said Molly.

"Um, I think ponies are scary," said Dinkin, honestly.

"Oh. What *do* you like?" asked Molly.

"I like being inside and making sure all the doors are locked," said Dinkin.

"If we were friends, you could play with all my toys and everything. And you could even play with Princess Puppy-Face if you liked! Do you want to be friends?"

Dinkin wasn't sure what to think about that. He wouldn't normally make friends with a little girl. Then again, he wouldn't normally make friends at all—he'd never actually had any friends other than The Frightening Things. He wondered what it might feel like. He also wondered how he could have imagined Molly was a zombalien. His mom and dad would be quick to say how stunningly silly he had been. He took the Zomb-O-Tron 6000 off his head, and put it on the floor. Fourteen seconds later, he said:

"I . . . think we could be friends . . ."

"Yay! We'll be the bestest friends ever!" said Molly, clapping her hands together. Dinkin suddenly felt incredibly awkward and, secretly, quite good.

"I'd better go. I don't want to get into trouble," said Dinkin.

"Do you want to come over and play tomorrow?" said Molly.

Dinkin thought for a moment. "I . . . suppose I could."

"Yay! What should we play? Ponies? Oh, wait, I have a better idea . . . ," she said, and she tore off her human disguise!

107

WHEN ZOMBALIENS ATTACK!

Danger of robot vampire attack: 0.0002%
Danger of snot monster attack: 0.013%
Danger of zombalien attack: 99.999%

Dinkin stared in frozen horror for the second time that night. He watched, terrified, as Molly threw her human disguise on the floor. Her skin was gray and rotting. Her huge eyes glowed red, and she had two wriggling antennae on the top of her head. Thick, white ooze dripped from her mouth, running between row upon row of yellow fangs. And she really did smell like sour milk and old ladies' underwear. She *was* a zombalien! Dinkin would have felt smug, if not for being more scared than he had ever been.

"I fooled you there for a second—admit it!" said Molly triumphantly. "What a performance! I even *cried*! I should get an Oscar!"

"AAAAHHHH!!!"

screamed Dinkin, tearing out of the bedroom.

"There's nowhere to run!" the zombalien cried, chasing after him. Dinkin raced down the corridor and into the first room he came across. It was Mr. and Mrs. Coddle's bedroom.

"Mr. Coddle! Mrs. Coddle! Wake up! Molly's a zombalien!" he screamed. Mr. and Mrs. Coddle sat bolt upright in bed.

"Well, of course she's a zombalien—she's our daughter, after all!" said the Coddles in unison, and tore off their human disguises!

"AAAAHHHH!!!"

screamed Dinkin.

"You're good, human, I'll give you that!" said Mr. Coddle. "No one's ever seen through a zombalien disguise before. Of course, Molly could only afford the basic disguise on her pocket money. The Mrs. and I upgraded to the

new I-Can't-Believe-It's-Not-Human Version 2.0!"

"It's even *more* impossible to see through! Touch it. It's just like the real thing!" drooled Mrs. Coddle, flinging her human mask at Dinkin. "And, you don't get any of the chafing you get from Version 1.0 . . . "

"V-v-very l-l-lifelike," stammered Dinkin.

"Are you both going to talk all night? There's zombifying to be done!" grumbled Molly. She growled an ooze-filled growl and turned her attention to a trembling Dinkin. "You know what, human? I was going to wait until the morning to zombify you, but since you're here now, it's brain eating time!"

"Don't worry, Duncan, life is *so* much better as a zombalien!" said Mrs. Coddle, with an ooze-filled grin. The three zombaliens gathered around Dinkin. As he felt their hot breath on his skin, Dinkin closed his eyes . . .

Suddenly, a pair of arms shot up through the floor and grabbed Dinkin by the ankles. He immediately turned ghostly and was pulled

into the floor below.

"Got him!" cried Arthur. He carried Dinkin down to the Coddles' kitchen, where the other Frightening Things were waiting.

"You all right, Dinkin?" said Herbert.

"Zombalien! Everyone's a zombalien!" screamed Dinkin, and then he noticed Edgar was missing his right arm. "Wait, what happened to you?"

"Do you mean after Princess Puppy-Face *pulled* off my arm or after we *finally* managed to wring all the water out of Arthur so he could make us ghostly and transport us safely inside?" said Edgar grumpily.

"Uh . . . nevermind," said Dinkin, hearing the zombaliens running downstairs. "Come on, we have to get out of here!"

Dinkin and The Frightening Things raced to the front door, the sound of brain-hungry zombaliens close behind. They were almost there when they spotted Princess Puppy-Face crouched on the floor. She was busily chewing on something.

"My arm!" shrieked Edgar. "She's eating my arm! You stinking little mutt, give that back!"

Princess Puppy-face got to her feet, let out a low snarl and began to shake. As Dinkin and The Frightening Things looked on in disbelief, she shook off her dog disguise! Her rotten, gray skin hung off her bones and her huge, red eyes lit up the darkness.

"Oh, for goodness' sake, is anyone around here *not* a zombalien?" said Dinkin.

The zombalien dog-beast snarled and started pacing toward them. Dinkin and The Frightening Things turned to run and came face-to-face with the drooling mouths of the three hungry zombaliens!

"There's nowhere left to run!" growled Molly. "Just one bite and you will be my zombie slave. First you, then your family, then the house across the street, then the next street, then the town, then the next town, then—"

"Oh, just bite him!" said Mrs. Coddle.

"Arthur, ghost us out of here!" cried Dinkin.

"What? Without my arm?" screeched Edgar. "I need that for . . . for . . . well, for all kinds of things!"

"There's no time! Arthur, make us ghostly, now!" yelled Dinkin.

"Too late, human!" screamed Molly, pouncing on Dinkin. She pinned him to the floor and opened her ooze-covered jaws to bite. But as her mouth touched Dinkin's neck . . .

"*Bleeehh!*" shrieked Molly. She fell to the floor, holding her stomach.

"What on earth's the matter with you? Honestly, Molly, you're *such* a picky eater!" said Mrs. Coddle. She grabbed Dinkin and tried to bite him.

"*Yuurk!*" she burped, and threw up all over the floor.

"It . . . it *can't* be!" said Mr. Coddle. He grabbed Dinkin, sniffed him, and gave him a cautious lick.

"BLURRRRRGH!!" he bawled, and spewed slime all over Dinkin's rain boots.

Dinkin couldn't believe his luck (besides the zombalien vomit on his boots—it was going to take at least six hours of scrubbing to get them clean again). He watched as the zombaliens rolled around the floor in agony. He lifted his arm, sniffed it, and then licked it. He recognized the taste immediately.

IT WAS THE TASTE OF FEAR.

THE TASTE OF FEAR

Number of embarrassing zombalien secrets revealed: 1

"What's going on?" said Herbert as the zombaliens continued to spew gray-green vomit all over the floor.

"I don't believe it," said Dinkin, climbing onto a chair to avoid the sea of vomit. "It seems like zombaliens are allergic to the one thing I have plenty of: fear!"

"You mean . . . ," began Edgar.

"I mean they can't stand the taste of fear! Which means they can't stand the taste of *me*!" cried Dinkin.

"You taste like nightmares!" said Molly, holding her stomach.

"I can't believe it's happening again," said Mr. Coddle.

"Silence! Do not reveal *The Secret*!"

"What secret? What's happening again? What are you talking about?" asked Dinkin.

Mr. and Mrs. Coddle looked at each other, and sighed.

"The thing is, we've been zombaliens for years, traveling from one planet to the next, trying to turn everyone into mindless zombie slaves," began Mrs. Coddle.

121

"But it's always the same! The minute we try to actually bite anyone, we feel terrible. We're allergic to fear!" said Mr. Coddle.

"But the trouble is, *everyone's* scared of zombaliens!" explained Mrs. Coddle. "I mean, just look at us—we're hideous and terrifying!"

"That does sound tricky. So why don't you just do something else?" asked Dinkin, actually starting to feel a little sorry for them.

122

"Like what? Zombifying is all we know," said Mr. Coddle.

"Well, you could be Frightening Things," said Edgar, re-attaching his arm.

"Oh, yes, we don't have to zombify *anyone*," said Arthur. "Plus, the hours are good and you get tons of holidays."

"We have been looking for a change of pace," said Mrs. Coddle.

"Don't listen to the human! We are zombaliens!" cried Molly.

"Oh, *please* be quiet, Molly," said Mrs. Coddle.

As it turned out, everyone ended up getting along pretty well (except for Molly, who was sulking). In fact, by the end of the night, the zombaliens had promised to abandon their plans for global zombification altogether. And Dinkin, in turn, promised to keep them and their rather embarrassing "fear allergy" a secret.

123

Before long, it was time for everyone to say their good-byes.

As the rain dried up, Dinkin and The Frightening Things snuck back to the house and slinked upstairs to Dinkin's bedroom. They made it back just in time to see the dawn light creep into the room.

"Well, good night, Dinkin," said Edgar. "And congratulations on a job well done."

"Thanks for the rescue. That was a close one, even for me," said Dinkin as he watched The Frightening Things fade into nothing. He was about to get into bed when there was a knock on his door. It was Dinkin's mother.

"Morning, Dinkin, up already? Oh, good! That gives you plenty of time to get ready for school."

JUST WHEN YOU THOUGHT IT WAS SAFE

Temperature: 61°F
Outlook: sunny and bright with a slight chance of horror

That morning at breakfast, Dinkin lazily shoveled cornflakes (soaked in milk for sixteen minutes to prevent gum-scraping) into his mouth. It was all he could do to stay awake.

"Jeez, Dink—you look like a zombie!" said Mr. Dings as he swigged his third cup of coffee. "Didn't get much sleep, eh? Well, don't say I didn't warn you."

"It wasn't my fault," said Dinkin, rubbing his eyes. He thought for a moment about telling his parents all about his night with the zombaliens . . . about the fact that he was right all along. But in the end, he just shook his head and decided not to mention it. Not only would they not believe him, but sometimes it was just easier if he dealt with things himself.

DING-DONG!

The doorbell! Dinkin jumped a foot in the air as he always did when the doorbell rang. Mrs. Dings got up to answer it. *Doorbells ringing at this hour?* Dinkin was immediately suspicious. He followed his mom at a safe distance and hid behind the coat rack as she opened the door. It was a man dressed as a mailman.

"Oh, hello," said the man dressed as a mailman. "I'm new to this route, so I thought I'd give you a ring-a-ding and say hello."

"Oh, how lovely! Nice to meet you. My name's Mrs. Dings," began Dinkin's mom, but Dinkin didn't hear any more. He took one look at the man dressed as a mailman and realized that he wasn't a mailman at all. He was something much, much more terrifying.

THIS WAS A JOB FOR THE FRIGHTENING THINGS!

LOOK OUT FOR DINKIN'S NEXT TERRIFYING ADVENTURE!